KU-674-807

SCRAP

First published 2015 by A & C Black,
an imprint of Bloomsbury Publishing Plc
50 Bedford Square, London, WC1B 3DP

www.bloomsbury.com

Bloomsbury is a registered trademark of Bloomsbury Publishing Plc

Copyright © A & C Black 2015
Text copyright © Judy Waite 2015
Illustrations © Ollie Cuthbertson 2015

The moral rights of the author have been asserted
All rights reserved

No part of this publication may be reproduced or transmitted by
any means, electronic, mechanical, photocopying or otherwise,
without the prior permission of the publishers

A CIP catalogue for this book is available from the British Library
ISBN: 978 1 4729 0938 1

Printed and bound in Great Britain by CPI Group (UK) Ltd,
Croydon, CR0 4YY

1 3 5 7 9 10 8 6 4 2

recommended by

www.catchup.org

Catch Up is a not-for-profit charity
which aims to address the problem of
underachievement that has its roots in
literacy and numeracy difficulties.

JUDY WAITE

Illustrated by
Ollie Cuthbertson

A & C BLACK
AN IMPRINT OF BLOOMSBURY
LONDON NEW DELHI NEW YORK SYDNEY

ST. HELENS COLLEGE
WAI
137200
Sept 2018
LIBRARY

Contents

Chapter One

Gangland

"Don't be long, there might be a rush of customers," Dad called.

Lewis was lugging the rubbish-bag to the back yard.

"And there might be aliens landing on the beach later tonight" Lewis muttered.

Their fish and chip shop had been open for three hours but hardly anyone had been in.

Dad was always waiting for a rush of customers in the shop. Always waiting – and always hoping.

Lewis walked over to the bins beside the high wooden gate. The gate was rotting. Some of the planks had broken and split. From further away, Lewis could hear waves crashing onto the beach. He had heard that sound all his life.

Just then, he heard footsteps in the alley behind the wooden gate.

"Hey loser, think that dog can beat mine?" said a rough voice.

"Just give him a chance," said a second voice. "He'll tear your dog's throat out!"

"Your dog couldn't beat mine. It's as weak as a kitten," said the first voice.

"You'll be sorry later, mate. You'll wish you hadn't said that."

"Not as sorry as you'll be," said the first voice.

Lewis stayed quiet. He could guess who was speaking. It was the older kids from the gangs. The gangs often hung out on the beach. Lewis and his dad hated them.

Dad hated the way they messed up the beach. They got drunk and left rubbish everywhere. Lewis hated how they treated their dogs: making them fight each other for fun. The dogs were bred for fighting and were very tough. The gangs treated them badly to wind them up. To make them dangerous.

"See you tomorrow." The first voice sounded angry. Threatening.

Lewis waited in the dark yard. There were old flower pots scattered about. Apart from the pots, and the bins, there was nothing there.

Lewis stood still. There was no sound from the ally.

They must have gone.

He dropped the rubbish into the bin. Just then, he heard a scuffling noise.

Someone was hiding behind the bins.

Chapter Two

Waiting Game

"Who's there?" Lewis called.

The scuffling stopped.

Lewis wished he hadn't left his mobile inside the chip shop. He could have called the police.

He had been texting Rachel White. She was

the most popular girl in his year at school. She'd messaged him about a party, but he couldn't go.

Dad needed him to work weekends in the summer holidays.

The scuffling started again.

"What do you want?" called Lewis, but there was no reply. The door of the chip shop was about ten steps away. He might have time to get inside and hit the alarm but then the police would come. A police car parked outside would be bad for business. It was no good. Lewis couldn't run away.

"OK then," he said softly. "If you won't come to me, then I'm coming for you."

He grabbed the nearest bin and wobbled it. A flowerpot tipped over with a clatter.

There was a yelp. Something small and brown sat hunched behind the bin.

"Hey!" The panic left Lewis. "You're a dog."

The dog's eyes bulged with fear. Lewis crouched level with it and held out his hand.

"Sniff me. You won't smell any danger," said Lewis.

He'd never had a dog. He'd never been allowed any pets. They lived in a tiny flat and Dad was always worried about germs getting into the fish and chip shop.

But Lewis knew you had to talk softly to a dog.

He knew you had to let animals catch your scent.

He kept his hand stretched out. The dog raised her head and sniffed.

Lewis didn't know much about dog-breeds. This dog looked a bit like the sort the gangs used for fighting, but she was smaller. Sweeter.

"Good dog. Come on, I won't hurt you," said Lewis.

The dog wagged her tail slowly. Lewis could see scabs and scars on her body.

Perhaps this wasn't a fighting dog, but some other dogs must have had a go at her.

She was probably a stray.

Maybe the gangs had made their dogs attack her. Lewis stroked her. He could feel her ribs.

"You're starving, aren't you? Hang on," he said.

He stood up and lifted the bin lid. Inside, was some soggy fish.

He crouched back down and he held a piece out.

The dog took it gently. First one piece, then another, and then another.

She looked at Lewis with dark, trusting eyes. Lewis scratched her neck and she rested against him.

Dad appeared in the back doorframe. "What on earth are you doing…?"

"Dad – I…"

Dad came striding out. "Why are you hiding by those bins?"

"Look at this little dog, Dad. I think she's been in a scrap, but she's really friendly. Just a bit scared. Could we…?"

Lewis's voice trailed away as his dad saw the dog for the first time.

"A dirty stray bringing in all sorts of diseases. Are you trying to poison our customers?" shouted Dad. He picked up one of the flower pots and threw it. It missed the dog, and smashed into pieces.

"Get lost, vermin. Don't bring your filthy fleas round here," Dad yelled again, waving his fist.

The dog didn't wait for Dad to have a second try at pot-throwing.

With a yelp, she scrambled through the gap in the gate and was gone.

Chapter Three

The Lie

Lewis got up early next morning. Dad was still asleep. He always slept late on Sundays.

Last night, there had been an ugly row about what Dad did to the dog.

Lewis knew that Dad would not talk to him for ages now. It was always like that after a row, and last night was the worst they had ever had.

The weather was warm already. Later, it would get really hot.

Lewis walked across the road and down the steps to the beach. He pushed his hands into his jacket pockets.

He wondered where the dog would be now. Perhaps Dad had scared her so much that she was still running.

Lewis walked past the pier, which stretched out over the sea. Waves lapped and slapped against its wooden posts. Then he walked up more steps that led to the coast path.

He decided he'd head on to the park. Perhaps he'd find the dog there. He could at least try and find someone who would look after her.

Five minutes later he reached the park.

"Hey, Lewis! Hi."

Lewis looked round. Rachel was walking towards him.

Her black and white dog jumped round her.

"Hi." Lewis stuck his hands even more deeply into his pockets.

He was always thinking about Rachel. He dreamed of asking her if she'd like to see a film, or go bowling. But whenever he saw her, he couldn't get his words out properly.

"What are you doing out so early?" asked Rachel. She pushed her gold-brown hair behind her ears. "Me and Patch usually have this park to ourselves this time of day."

Lewis wasn't sure what to tell her. Rachel's life was so different to his.

She lived in one of the posh houses on the edge of town. Her Mum had an important job in the city. Her Dad owned the local newspaper.

And they had a dog that they all adored.

How could he tell her about his row with Dad?

"I just needed some fresh air," Lewis mumbled at last. "The stink of fish and chips gets to me sometimes. It's always in our flat, even when we're not frying downstairs in the shop."

As soon as he'd said it, he knew it was the wrong thing to say.

No girl was going to go for someone whose home stunk of fish.

Patch ran over and licked Lewis's fingers.

"Stop it, Patch," Rachel giggled. "He's a bit over-friendly sometimes. But it means he likes you!" She smiled.

Lewis began to smile back and then remembered he hadn't cleaned his teeth yet. Gross! He put his hand over his mouth.

He was making an idiot of himself.

"Have you got any pets?" Rachel was still smiling.

"Yep. I've got a dog too." Lewis didn't know what made him say it. He just wanted her to think they had something in common.

"Have you?" Rachel's smile widened. "Is it with you now?"

"She ran away, just last night." Lewis was trying his best not to mumble. "That's why I'm out here this early. I'm trying to find her."

"Oh no – I'd be in a real state if Patch went missing. What's her name?"

Lewis hesitated. He remembered how the dog had been huddled behind the rubbish bin. He remembered the scabs and scars on her body. He remembered thinking she'd been in a scrap. "She's called Scrap," Lewis said suddenly. Somehow, giving the dog a name made his story seem more real. It made it feel as though Scrap really were his.

"Shall I help you look for her?" said Rachel.

Lewis hesitated. If he agreed to let her help, he'd have the whole morning with her. But then they'd be looking for a dog he didn't own.

A dog that wouldn't come to the name Scrap, even if they found her. "It's OK," he shrugged. "Scrap's a bit shy. I'll look for her by myself."

He walked away, knowing he'd been rude. And also knowing that, when she found out he had lied, she would never talk to him again.

Chapter Four

New Boy in Town

Lewis stood on the beach. The waves
sparkled in the warm sunlight. There was a man
and a small boy down by the water. The boy was
collecting shells in a bucket.

Lewis remembered doing that with Dad. They used to collect shells and stones and old glass that the sea had worn smooth. The glass was the best thing to find. It looked like jewels in the sunlight. Lewis used to call it his 'pirate treasure'. He still had some of it in his bedroom drawer.

Summers were great then. The chip shop was always busy and Dad was always happy. As Lewis got older, Dad let him help out in the shop. He'd been proud to do it.

Then, the chip shop stopped making money. Now, helping Dad felt more like being a slave than a son.

"Hi Lewis, are you still looking for poor Scrap?" Rachel called, as she walked up behind him. She was with a boy Lewis hadn't seen before.

"Um – yep. I've looked everywhere, but no luck."

Lewis hated all this lying. He wished he could run down into the sea and swim away from everyone. He would vanish and never be seen again.

Rachel turned to the boy. "Lewis has lost his dog."

"That's bad news," said the boy.

"This is Matt. He's moved into the house up the road from mine," Rachel smiled at Matt and Matt grinned back at her.

Lewis felt his gut lurch. They looked so happy together.

"Matt starts school with us in September. He'll be in our tutor group."

"That's good," Lewis said. "Cool."

His voice came out flat and empty.

He would have to watch Rachel and Matt together, day after day. She was bound to go for someone like him.

Lewis scratched Patch's ears so that he didn't have to look at Rachel.

Rachel was still talking. "Do you fancy meeting up later? Me and Matt are going bowling this afternoon."

The idea of going bowling with Rachel and Matt was even worse than the idea of watching them at school together. Matt would be a brilliant bowler. He would be brilliant at everything.

Lewis looked back towards the man and the little boy. They were paddling now. The boy was laughing as he jumped and splashed between the waves.

"Sorry," grunted Lewis, still scratching Patch's ears. "My dad needs me in the chip shop. I have to go back soon."

"You work on a Sunday?" asked Matt, and Lewis suddenly wanted to punch him. What did this posh geek know about chip shops? There were accounts to sort out. There was endless cleaning. There were always things to get ready before the next day.

"Yep." Lewis's voice wasn't flat anymore. It sounded angry.

Rachel glanced between Lewis and Matt. She looked puzzled for a moment, but then she smiled at Lewis again. "Come to our barbecue next Saturday. It's a welcome party for Matt and his family."

"No, I don't want to come to your poxy barbecue." The words were out before Lewis could help himself. He turned away and started running. He raced into the sea, splashing past the man and the little boy. He waded in right up to his chest.

He didn't look back to see if Rachel and Matt were watching him. He had been rude to her about looking for Scrap, but what he'd said this time was worse.

He started swimming.

Perhaps he really would swim away, and never be seen again.

Chapter Five

Dog's Dinner

Lewis didn't swim away. He kept level
with the shore. It wasn't easy swimming with his
clothes on, but he was a strong swimmer and he
was used to the sea. He'd lived by it all of
his life.

When he got past the pier Lewis looked to see if Rachel and Matt had gone. Then he waded back to the shore.

His clothes stuck to him. His trainers squelched.

"Mr Drippy! You look pathetic." A tall teenager stepped out from under the pier.

He had metal studs in his nose. Another boy followed. He had a sand-brown dog with him. The dog had a huge head, and massive jaws. Lewis was glad to see it was wearing a muzzle and a chain.

A girl appeared. She giggled at Lewis. "Did you just try to drown yourself, or something?"

"No," said Lewis and he moved to walk past, but Dog-boy blocked his path.

The dog slobbered. It clearly thought Lewis was its lunchtime snack.

"You know you have to pay to walk past us?" Metal-man grinned.

"We're the Beach Patrol," the girl giggled again.

"I haven't any money," said Lewis, trying to stop his voice from shaking.

"Hope you're not telling us fibs, Drippy. Cuddles here is trained to sniff out wallets, credit cards and money. You got anything like that on you?" Dog-boy jerked the chain.

The dog growled.

"No." Lewis swallowed hard.

It was true. He hadn't even brought his mobile. It was in his room, on the table by his bed.

"Maybe we should let Cuddles check you over, just to be sure." said Dog-boy. "It's easy to forget the odd soggy tenner that might be tucked in your back pocket." He jerked the chain again.

Metal-man gripped Lewis's chin. "Make it easy for yourself, Drippy" he said. "Remember – we've got a job to do. Beach Patrol!"

"I… I haven't got anything." Lewis wasn't normally a wimp but this was three against one – four if you counted the dog. If they laid into him, he wouldn't have a chance.

Metal-man pushed his thumb up under Lewis's eye.

Lewis wondered if his eye would pop out. Would a little boy find it and put it in his bucket with his shells?

"Time to remove Cuddles's muzzle, don't you think, Drippy?" Dog-boy sneered.

Then, there was a shout. "Leave him alone!"

Matt was running down the steps from the path.

Lewis felt sick. Things would get worse now. Matt would wind the gang up. Any second now Dog-boy would rip the muzzle from the dog, and it would be 'game-over'.

'Death by Dog'. Lewis wondered if the story would make the papers. Maybe Rachel's dad would print it.

Matt stopped just out of the gang's reach. "You know that dog is illegal?"

"Illegal?" the girl smirked. "Why?"

"Your dog is illegal," said Matt. "It's a Japanese Tosa. They're dangerous. They've been bred for fighting and they don't know any better. See my mate up there?"

Lewis saw Rachel up on the coast path. Patch sat beside her.

Matt kept talking. "She's rung the police.
I'm sure that dog cost you a lot of money. If you
want to keep it, you'd better go. If you stay, not
only will you lose your – er – your lovely pet, but
you will get a mega fine. And probably a prison
sentence too."

The gang looked at each other. Then, Dog-boy
jerked the chain. "Come on Cuddles. Lunch is
off," he muttered. The three of them walked away.

"You OK?" Matt frowned at Lewis.

The sun was still shining but Lewis's teeth
were chattering. "Just about."

"Normally I'd have reported a Japanese Tosa
and given the police a chance to get here," said
Matt. "But it didn't look like there was any time
to spare."

"No. Probably not."

"We'll walk you home." Matt waved at Rachel.

Lewis shook his head "No. It's OK. I'll be fine." He knew he needed to be thankful to Rachel and Matt, but he couldn't let Rachel see him shaking like a scared rabbit.

At least Rachel had made the right choice. Matt was perfect for her. He even knew about Japanese Toe-Dogs, or whatever they were called.

He walked away, hoping Matt would think it was the salt and sand bringing tears to his eyes.

Chapter Six

Pirate Patter

He expected Dad to shout at him. He expected him to go on about how he couldn't run the shop on his own.

But, as Lewis walked into the chip shop, Dad gave him a long, slow look. "You seem a bit shaken up lad," he said, in a soft voice. One that Lewis had not heard him use for a long time. "Go and get showered. Relax a bit."

Lewis showered and changed. Then he sat on his bed.

He took the pirate-treasure glass from his drawer and dropped it onto his quilt.

"Ah ha there, Lewis lad!" Dad walked into the bedroom. He was talking in his 'pirate voice' and winking. That was the way he used to talk when they brought the glass home and washed it. "I see treasure ahoy."

Lewis looked up at him. "Not sure why I've kept it all this. It's stupid really."

Dad picked up a piece of green glass. "It brings back good memories." He sat down on the bed. "I wish we could go back to those days when everything was going well."

Lewis chose a square of gold-brown glass and lifted it up. He looked through it. His whole bedroom went golden brown.

"Look Lewis, I know I work you hard, but we need money so you can go to college," said his dad. "You need to train. You need to get qualified."

"I don't want to go to college." Lewis kept on looking through the gold-brown glass. "I'm not good at anything."

"You know about customers. You can cook. You know how a business works," his dad smiled.

Lewis dropped the gold-brown glass down onto the bed. That was the trouble. He knew Dad was right, but he didn't want to do jobs like that when he left school.

Dad put his glass down next to Lewis's. His voice was gritty, as if he suddenly had sand it his throat. "Whatever you decide to do, I will be right behind you," he said. "But I want you to know that I'm grateful for all the help you give here."

Lewis was about to mumble "thanks" when his mobile rang.

Dad picked it up and read the name that flashed up on the screen.

RACHEL

He handed the phone to Lewis.

Lewis pushed it away. "I'll call her later."

But before he knew what was happening, Dad was answering his phone. "Lewis is busy at the moment, can I take a message?"

Lewis mouthed the words "no, Dad," but Dad ignored him.

Lewis could hear Rachel's voice but couldn't hear what she was saying. He put his head into his hands.

"A barbecue? Both of us invited? I'm afraid I can't make it. Saturday is our busiest night. But…" Dad turned and winked at Lewis. "… Lewis can come. I'll get a temp to help in the shop."

Lewis groaned. What excuse could he have now? Rachel and Matt had rescued him from the gang on the beach. He couldn't snub them again. He'd have to stand around being polite to strangers. Even worse he would have to watch while Rachel and Matt had a great time together.

Chapter Seven

Temp Trouble

The evening of the barbecue arrived. Lewis kept as busy as possible. He didn't look at the time.

"You should have left for that barbecue by now." Dad frowned as Lewis mixed fresh batter and dipped in more fish.

"The shop's busy. I can't just leave you. Not now that the temp hasn't turned up," said Lewis.

"She was stuck in traffic half an hour ago. She should be here in a minute," said Dad.

Lewis put chips into the fryer. He was pleased the temp was stuck in traffic. He'd been dreading the barbecue all week.

He turned to the next customer. "Good evening. What can I get you?"

Dad nudged him out the way. "Leave it Lewis. Just get going!"

"This is our busiest night for years, Dad. Customers won't come back if we keep them waiting…"

"I said I'll deal with it." Dad was managing to smile at the customer and glare at Lewis at the same time. "If you don't leave now, I'll shut the shop and drive you there myself."

"What, and leave the customers to serve themselves?" Lewis shook his head.

"A taxi then. I'll order you a taxi," said Dad.

"Brilliant. Let's spend the night's profits on getting me there."

Dad scowled.

"Anyway Dad, I can't go. It's a posh party. Apart from anything else, I'm going to smell like a..." He stopped, trying to think of the best words. "...like a fish and chip shop," he muttered.

Dad looked at him, and Lewis knew he understood. Stinking of fish and chips was something they both had to live with.

Dad sighed. "Well I suppose..."

The shop door opened. "Oh, Mr Rymer, I'm so, so sorry. I drove as fast as I could. I'm Molly, by the way." A middle-aged blonde woman pushed her way through the line of customers. "Right. Now tell me what you need me to do," she said, pulling on her apron.

Dad grinned at Lewis and winked. "There you are Lewis lad. I reckon you can be out of this place all clean and fresh in less than fifteen minutes."

Chapter Eight

Race Against the Tide

Lewis was late. He hated the idea of turning up half way through the party. Now, he just wanted to get there. He wanted to eat a super-posh-steak-burger, and then leave.

He could be back at the chip shop before Dad even closed up. They could pay Molly the temp for her time and get rid of her. Why pay Molly when Lewis could do the work? He would be faster, and better. Then, Lewis laughed. He was sounding just like Dad. Dad was always fussing about money and getting jobs done. Perhaps he'd make a decent businessman after all!

It was still light, but the moon was already out: a full moon. That meant an extra high tide.

Lewis hurried along the coast path. He looked out at the sea. The water hadn't covered the beach yet, but it was rolling up fast.

A movement under the pier caught his eye. It looked as though there were two people down there.

He wondered if he should go and tell them it wasn't safe. A lot of people didn't know how quickly the sea could flood in. But then he saw that it was Metal-man and that girl: two of those thugs from the beach last weekend.

They went under the pier again.

The girl's silly giggle rang up the beach. Metal-man was laughing too. Lewis could hear glass smashing. He guessed they were chucking empty bottles about. Lewis wondered if they were drunk. A moment later they appeared on the other side of the pier, stumbling away.

Lewis was about to walk on when a new sound reached him. This sound was quite small. A thin, scared sound.

It was a dog barking.

Lewis thought at first that Dog-boy must be down there too.

He must have taken the muzzle off the Japanese Toe-Dog. But Lewis was sure the Japanese Toe-Dog's bark would be louder. And fiercer.

The barks seemed to be coming from under the pier.

He glanced back along the beach. Metal-man and the girl were a long way off now. The barking was more frantic. The dog sounded scared. He couldn't just leave it to suffer.

He raced down the steps and ran towards the shore.

A little brown dog was crouched under the pier, looking out at him. Lewis recognised her straight away. It was the stray he'd found in his back yard. It was Scrap.

Chapter Nine

Trapped

"Hey Scrap, remember me?" said Lewis. Then he saw what Metal-man and the girl had done to Scrap. They'd tied her by the neck to one of the posts under the pier. The tide was already lapping at her paws.

The string was knotted tight. It was cutting into Scrap's skin.

Scrap's tail wagged nervously. The sea rolled in again and splashed over Lewis's trainers.

"I'm going to get this off you." Lewis twisted the string. It bit into his fingers but he couldn't break it.

Scrap wagged her tail again. "Brave girl." Lewis knew that every time he pulled the string, it tightened round her throat.

He pushed his hand into his jeans pocket. He'd call Dad and get someone to bring a knife. But his mobile wasn't there. Lewis remembered it was in the pocket of his other jeans: the ones that were in a heap on his bedroom floor, stinking of fish and chips.

The sea rose higher. Lewis knew how fast the tide would come in. Soon the waves would cover Scrap.

Lewis realised he was crying and he didn't try to stop. He put his arms round Scrap. The waves rolled over her. She blinked the water out of her eyes, watching Lewis. She trusted him. He couldn't see if her tail was wagging anymore. He held her close as the water surged round them.

"I'm sorry," he sobbed. "I'm so sorry."

Then, he saw a gold-brown beer bottle floating by. It was broken and the jagged edges stuck up out of the water. It reminded Lewis of the broken glass he had collected with Dad. He had called it pirate treasure all those years ago. Now, this bottle was a different sort of treasure. He could use its jagged edges to save Scrap's life.

The water swelled against his waist.

Lewis grabbed the bottle and held Scrap's head above water.

He held the jagged edge against the string.

Lewis was an expert with knives. He could strip a fish from its bone. He knew how to angle a blade. He knew how hard to press.

He rubbed and sliced. It still wasn't working.

Lewis spat as a new wave splashed across his face. It washed up over his shoulders. He had to stay steady. He could slit Scrap's throat if he got this wrong.

Then, the string snapped.

Scrap was free.

"Swim, Scrap!" Lewis pushed her towards the shore. Scrap paddled. The tide pushed her forward, rolling her to safety. "That's great, Scrap, you're…" Lewis shouted. But he didn't finish his sentence.

Another giant wave rolled in, knocking him off his feet. He felt his head crack as the wave bashed his head against the pier-post.

Chapter Ten

Losing Hope

Lewis tried to swim upwards but he seemed to be spinning.

Opening his eyes, he could make out the blurry shape of the pier-post. He stretched forward to grip it. The post felt slimy and was slippery with seaweed.

The water seemed to be rocking him. It was a gentle feeling. "Maybe I'll just stay here?" he murmured to himself. "Maybe there isn't any need to swim to the surface after all?" He let himself float down, and down, and down. And then he heard a sound, far away above the waves.

Scrap was barking. Lewis wasn't dizzy anymore and he scrabbled wildly, moving up the post.

As he hit the surface of the water, he could see Scrap on the beach. She was racing madly, first one way and then the other. She kept barking.

Lewis knew he needed to swim towards her, but he wasn't sure he had the strength to make it to the shore. His head was screaming with pain. If he let go of the post he might just go under again. The sea was so deep now. He was almost out of his depth.

He wondered how long the dog could keep barking. "Go home, Scrap," he murmured. "You can't help."

And then he remembered that Scrap didn't have a home. He wondered where she went when she got too tired to race up and down.

The pain in his head made it hard to think, but he had to keep awake. If he went to sleep, he would never wake up.

He made himself think about different things. Things from long ago. He remembered swimming here with Dad. They used to have races from this pier.

Later, they'd have ice cream. Lewis's favourite had a lemony flavour. He could almost taste it now.

The sea pulled at him. He was losing his grip. He tried to hold tighter.

He thought about ice creams again. Dad always went for a 99. Lewis used to nick the chocolate out of the ice cream. Dad would pretend to be cross with him. He used to talk like a pirate. "Oi there young Lewis lad. I'll make you walk the plank if you don't give that back."

"Oi, Lewis! Oi, Lewis!"

It was as if Dad were really with him now. "Thanks for everything, Dad," he whispered. He wasn't going to be able to hold on much longer.

"Oi, Lewis! Oi, Lewis!"

And then Lewis realised that what he was hearing wasn't in his mind.

"Lewis? Lewis?" It really was Dad's voice. It was coming from the beach and was all mixed up with Scrap's barking.

Lewis could hear Rachel too. "Lewis? Where are you? Can you hear us?"

"Dad! Rachel!" Lewis waved, splashing madly.

"OK lad – we see you. We're coming onto the pier to throw you a life-ring."

Chapter Eleven

Hard Choices

Rachel didn't seem to mind the smell of fish and chips in their flat after all. She and Dad fussed around Lewis, getting him hot chocolate and blankets.

Scrap lay across Lewis's feet.

"That dog saved you," Dad said for the millionth time. "If she hadn't kept on barking, we wouldn't have known where to look."

"I got worried when you didn't turn up," Rachel explained. "I couldn't get an answer from your mobile so I rang the chip shop. Your Dad said you'd left ages ago."

"Once Rachel told me the gang story, I was frantic," Dad butted in. "Rachel met me on the path. It was her who thought the barking might be something to do with you and your 'lost dog'."

Lewis felt his face flush red. "Sorry about that," he mumbled. "Sorry I lied."

Rachel smiled. "I used to tell people I had a horse. I never have had one – my dad says it would take up too much time. He says it would affect my school work." She looked round at Dad. "He wants me to be a doctor."

Dad nodded. "Parents are like that. We want our children to do well."

Molly appeared at the door. "Everything's sorted in the shop now. I can do shifts next week, too, if Lewis isn't up to it." She smiled at Lewis's dad and Lewis's dad smiled back.

Lewis looked at Rachel and raised his eyebrows. They both struggled not to giggle.

"And this little superstar?" Molly said, pointing at Scrap. "Are you going to keep her?"

Lewis shook his head. "It wouldn't be fair. She would be stuck upstairs all day when I'm at school. But could we try and find a good home. Somewhere I can visit?"

Rachel looked excited. "You remember Matt – the boy you met last week?"

Lewis's heart sank. He'd been wondering how long it would take before Matt's name came up. He didn't think he could bear it if Matt had Scrap. "Yep. I remember him," he said.

"His dad is a vet and they've moved here to set up a dog rescue shelter. Matt and his girlfriend are helping. I'm sure they'd take Scrap. I can ask my dad to put the story in his paper, too. I bet lots of people will offer Scrap a good home."

Lewis stroked Scrap's back. He liked the idea of lots of people offering her a good home. He could check them out and choose the best.

As he thought about that, he realised Rachel had said something else too. She'd said Matt had a girlfriend. He and Rachel were only mates.

Lewis looked at Rachel, and Rachel looked at Lewis. They smiled.

This time it was Dad and Molly's turn to raise their eyebrows!

SEATOWN NEWS

STRAY DOG SAVES DROWNING BOY

Local boy, Lewis Rymer, owes his life to a small stray dog. When Lewis was almost drowning in the sea the dog ran up and down barking, raising the alarm.

"She's a real star," said Lewis, whose father runs the 'Sea View Fish 'n Chip' shop on Beach Street.

The dog, now named Scrap, has been taken in by the dog shelter at Shore Lane. "We were planning to re-home her," said Rachel White, who works as a volunteer, "but we've all fallen in love with her. So now she has a permanent home here. She's our mascot."

"Scrap not only saved my life, but she changed it," Lewis explained. "I've been accepted as a volunteer here at the rescue centre. I never knew what I wanted to do in life, but Scrap has helped me decide. I'm going to train to work with dogs."

SHORE LANE SHELTER
Autumn Fete
10.30am
Saturday 3 September
ALL WELCOME

The rescue centre aims to not only rescue and re-home strays but to raise public awareness about the dangers of dog fighting, and in particular the owning of banned breeds such as the Pit Bull Terrier and the Japanese Tosa.